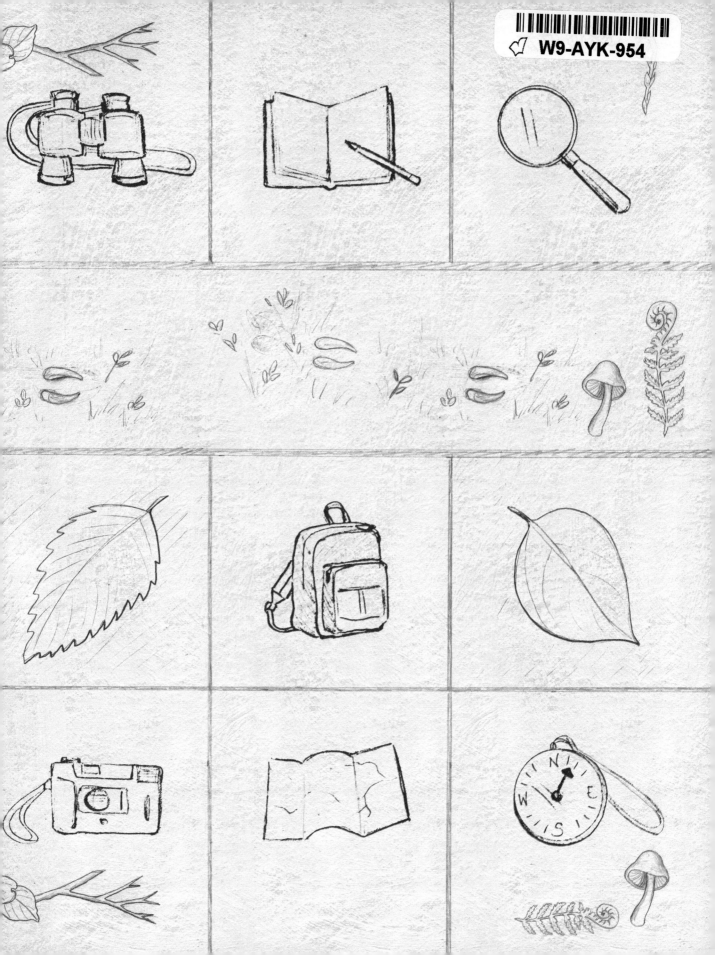

Special thanks to:

Lois Bradley for true friendship and advice.

Grace Roff for her mad-helpful computer skills.

Melissa Turk for her devotion to the birth of this book.

Designed by Neecy Twinem of Painted Sky Studio, Inc.
neecytwinem.com
Edited by Theresa Howell

Published by Muddy Boots
An imprint of Globe Pequot
MuddyBootsBooks.com

Distributed by NATIONAL BOOK NETWORK

British Library Cataloguing-in-Publication Information available
Library of Congress Cataloging-in-Publication Data available

ISBN 978-1-63076-308-4 (hardcover)
ISBN 978-1-63076-309-1 (e-book)

Printed in India, November 2021

My Hike in the Forest

written and illustrated by

Neecy Twinem

Look for the animal tracks on each spread
that will lead you to the ending.

muddy boots

we jump in puddles

Down the soft path and into the lush forest, we eagerly begin our hike. All is quiet, but we know the woods are full of life. What will we encounter today—birds, flowers, maybe even a deer?

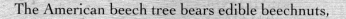

The American beech tree bears edible beechnuts,

Native Americans used the bark and roots of the dogwood for medicine.

Over our heads, tall beech and oak trees reach to the sky with their tiny leaves.
Scattered underneath, small dogwood trees burst with pretty white blossoms.
Why is it called a dogwood? I wonder.

The dogwood has scarlet autumn foliage.

which are eaten by wildlife.

Birds love to eat the red berries of the dogwood in autumn.

Female spiders lay eggs.

Spiders build webs to catch their prey.

According to Navajo folklore, weavers learned their trade from spiders.

We spy a sparkling spiderweb delicately clinging between two branches. Looking closer, we see the colorful orb spider waiting patiently for its prey. Let's leave her alone and continue down the trail.

Near our feet, we see green moss. We stop to stroke the soft, cushiony mounds speckled with star-shaped buds.

The moss case is full of spores that must mature.

Ferns are one of the oldest groups of plants on Earth.

Feathery ferns surround
us with curly new leaves,
unrolling as they grow.
Fiddleheads!

The fully opened leaves are called fronds.

Below us, we hear the dry leaves on the ground move. We freeze. Oh! It's a garter snake slithering out to show its pretty stripes. I breathe a sigh of relief and we carry on.

Snakes stick out their tongues to pick up smells and to feel things.

Garter snakes eat toads.

Garter snakes eat salamanders.

Garter snakes eat earthworms.

Garter snakes eat frogs.

Trilliums and Indian pipes need the rich humus of the forest floor.

Native Americans once gathered trilliums for medicine.

Earthworms and pill bugs feed on plant matter,

Around the bend, the woodland floor
is covered with flowers. It is a sweet
smelling carpet of white and green.
Trilliums form triangles with their
three white petals and large leaves.
The Indian pipe flowers look like little
pipes popping out of the damp earth.

Trilliums make red berries after the flowers fade.

making the soil rich for plants to grow.

Above my head I hear a happy song.
Chewy-chewy-chewy, chew-chew-chew.
We look up to see the brilliant orange and black
American redstart.
Chewy-chewy-chewy, chew-chew-chew,
we answer back.

Redstarts can hover in midair.

The redstart makes its cup-like nest out of grasses, bark, and spider's silk.

This bird eats flying insects that it catches in midair.

There is a rustling sound ahead of us.
Is it a deer?
NO. A furry, striped chipmunk scurries out
of the undergrowth and up onto a big rock.
I smile as it sits gazing at us
with dark eyes.

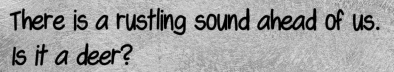

berries, and insects.

These are chipmunk tracks.

and sounds the alarm of "chip-chip" when predators are near.

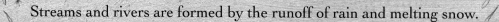

Streams and rivers are formed by the runoff of rain and melting snow.

Plants use water and release water back into the forest.

Our path winds around a bend to the lively sound of a trickling stream. We stop to touch the cool water and count the different colors of lichen that coat the rocks along the banks. Is that a pair of eyes bulging out of the shallow water?

 Lichen is a type of plant with no roots, stem, or leaves.

Streams are the arteries of the forest.

Animals drink water and return it to the forest through their waste.

Lichens are found on rocks and trees, but get their nutrients from the air.

Baby frogs are called tadpoles.

Frogs hatch from eggs.

Frogs are shiny and smooth.

Tadpoles will grow legs and lose their tails.

Frogs eat numerous insects which they grab with their tongue.

I take a step closer. Whoops! Up leaps a smooth, wet pickerel frog! It splashes our legs as it jumps through the water.

The skin gland secretions of the pickerel frog make them distasteful to predators.

Woodpeckers make their nests in the holes of old trees.

A tapping sound echoes through the trees. High over our heads, we see the black and white markings of a red-bellied woodpecker. He is busy tapping into the hard bark of the tree.

Woodpeckers peck and dig to eat insects from the trunk of trees.

Woodpeckers talk to their mates by "drumming" on trees.

by wedging them in the bark of trees.

Turkeys make their nest on the ground with leaves and grasses.

Farther down the path we spot some large wild turkeys foraging on the ground. One of the birds spreads its tail feathers like a fan.

Wild turkeys eat seed, insects, and fruit.

 Some Native American tribes believed the turkey to be magical,

The hen may have as many as 15 eggs in her nest to care for.

Before we can get any closer,
they disappear into
the woods, gobbling as they go.

Male turkeys strut and display their feathers to get attention from females.

and they adorned themselves with turkey feathers.

Cottontails have big eyes to see danger coming.

Baby rabbits are called kittens.

Our trail leads into a large, grassy clearing. There sits a cottontail rabbit quietly munching on young plants. Its ears shift back and forth, and in a split second, it hops away with a flash of its fluffy tail.

Cottontails have big, sharp teeth to chomp on grasses,

Cottontails have large ears that move around and listen for danger.

These are the tracks of a cottontail rabbit.

fruit, and other plants.

Mushrooms are fungi and come in many different colors and shapes.

Mushrooms are found in shady, damp places.

When threads from two mushrooms join under the ground,

Back in the trees, we stop to rest in the cool shade near an old stump dressed in thick orange-red fungus. At its base is a cluster of creamy white mushrooms. As we sit, we suddenly sense something nearby.

Deer have a thick fur coat to insulate them against water and cold.

Every spring, male deer grow a new pair of antlers

Deer feed on a wide variety of plants and twigs.

We turn our heads and find ourselves face-to-face with a white-tailed deer! In a fleeting moment it turns and bounds away into the shelter of the trees. We smile, wondering what other marvels await us on our hike through the forest.

These are the tracks of a white-tailed deer.

and shed them in the fall.

My Hike in the Forest
Scavenger Hunt

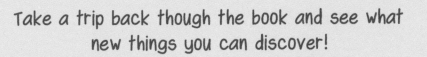

Take a trip back though the book and see what
new things you can discover!

The deer was hiding on four different pages. Did you find them all?

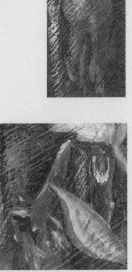

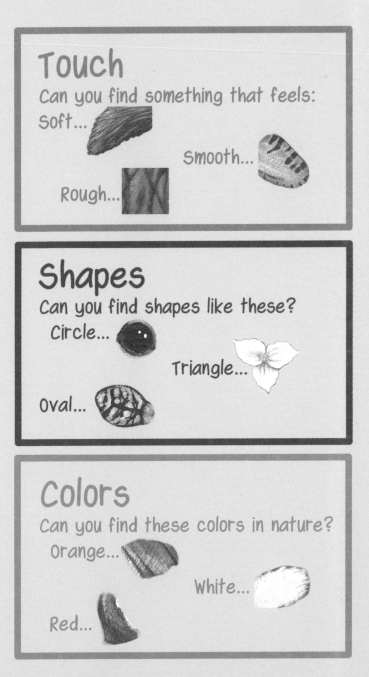

Touch
Can you find something that feels:
Soft...

Smooth...

Rough...

Shapes
Can you find shapes like these?
Circle...

Triangle...

Oval...

Colors
Can you find these colors in nature?
Orange...

White...

Red...

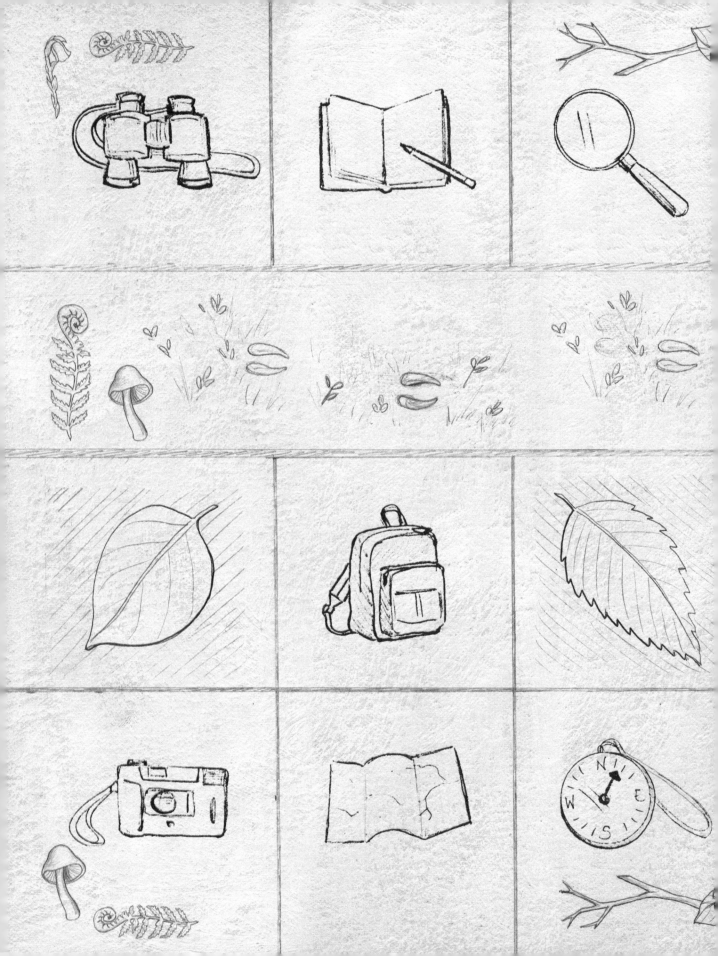